D0709643

Happy Holidays

PIXAR8350313

Bath · New York · Cologne · Melbourne · Delhi
Hong Kong · Shenzhen · Singapore

It was almost Christmas time, and Andy was playing in his room with his toys. In one hand he held Woody the cowboy, and in the other was Buzz Lightyear the space ranger.

"You're spending Christmas in jail!" Andy said in Woody's voice.

Andy's mother came into the room and sat down.

"Andy, I have a surprise for you," she said. "For your Christmas present this year . . . we're going to the Grand Canyon!"

"That's the best present ever!" Andy cried, dropping his toys and jumping up and down with excitement. "Can Buzz and Woody come, too?"

"I think it's better if you leave them here," Andy's mother said. "You'll be much too busy to play."

JAIL

As soon as Andy and his mother left the room, the toys came to life.

"All right!" Rex the dinosaur said. "The trip is Andy's Christmas present. That means no new toys to take our place!"

"Sure, that's great," Woody said. "But it also means Christmas without Andy."

"We'll just make it a toy Christmas!" Buzz said.

Woody forced a smile. He knew that Christmas without Andy just wouldn't be the same.

After Andy and his family left, the toys started getting ready for Christmas. They made decorations, sang carols, and looked for presents for each other. Jessie found Bullseye's missing red bandanna behind a stack of books.

"This is going to make a great Christmas present for Bullseye," Jessie grinned.

Later, Woody found Wheezy the penguin singing Christmas songs with Mike the tape recorder. He hoped the songs would put him in the Christmas spirit, but instead they just made him think of Andy.

Woody was glad his friends were in the holiday spirit, but he couldn't stop thinking about how much he missed Andy.

Over on the other side of the room, Woody found Slinky Dog and the Aliens decorating a Christmas tree made out of cotton balls. There were lots of colorful presents under the tree.

Woody couldn't help smiling. He was impressed that all the toys were working together to make Christmas a happy holiday.

On Christmas Eve, Buzz found Woody sitting by the window on his own.

"Why so down, Sheriff?" Buzz asked.

"Christmas Eve just isn't the same without Andy," Woody said sadly.

"You're right, it's not the same," said Buzz, putting his arm around Woody's shoulders. "But you have other friends besides Andy. Now, come with me. I want to show you something."

Woody and Buzz walked past Bo Peep. She was reading a Christmas story to the newest toys. It was their first Christmas, and their faces were all lit up with smiles.

Bo winked at Woody, and his heart suddenly felt a bit lighter.

THE NIGHT BEFORE CHRISTMAS

Buzz led Woody over to the Christmas tree.

"Here's a little thing I like to call Christmas magic," Buzz said.

He pressed the laser button on his right arm, and a beam of light shot out onto the wall. The light created a dazzling show of snowflakes, sugarplums, and toys. Woody's jaw dropped and his eyes grew wide.

"Wow, Buzz!" he said. "That's amazing!"

Just then, RC rolled over, all decorated to look like a sleigh. Rex followed behind—dressed as Santa Claus!

Rex began handing the Christmas presents out to every toy. Bullseye was thrilled to have his bandanna back. Mr. Spell got new batteries, Hamm got a shiny coin, and one of the dolls gave Jessie a dress.

Finally, Bo Peep gave Woody a big kiss. His cheeks turned as red as the Christmas lights.

"Hey, everyone!" Slinky Dog yelled from the window. "Check this out!"

He opened the curtains. It was starting to snow.

"Merry Christmas, everyone!" he shouted.

Woody looked at his friends and smiled. Buzz was right. Christmas without Andy wasn't any better or worse. It was just different. Spending time with the people—and toys—you loved was what Christmas was all about.

Bo Peep gives Woody a kiss under the mistletoe.

Buzz and Woody are having a snowball fight!

Bullseye helps Jessie the cowgirl put a star on top of the tree.

Stretch is decorating the Christmas tree.
How many ornaments can you count in his tentacles?
Write your answer in the box below.

Stretch has ☐ ornaments.

ANSWER: 8

The best present of all is friendship.

Hamm and Jessie love making Christmas cookies.
Draw some cookies on the tray for them to decorate.

The Green Army Men make sure all the stockings are hung correctly.

The Roundup gang are all in the holiday spirit! Find and circle six differences in the bottom image.

ANSWER:

Lightning McQueen and Mater like to race in the snow.

Mater helps hang a Christmas wreath.

Guido places the star at the top of the Christmas tree.

TJ tries ice skating, but he thinks the ice is too cold!

Lightning and Sally admire the view from up top.
It's a winter wonderland!

Lightning McQueen gets a brand new set of tires.
What a great gift!

Ramone makes some beautiful snow-cars!

Guido and Luigi are ready for a snowball fight!

Riley is so excited about Christmas!

Joy can't wait to find out what Riley will
get from Santa Claus this year. . . .
Draw what she's imagining in the thought bubble.

Disgust loves everything about the holidays . . .
except ugly Christmas sweaters! Eww!

Riley likes to play hockey
during the holidays.

Riley and her family can't wait to celebrate the holidays together in their new home. Can you spot and circle nine things that are different in the bottom picture?

ANSWER:

"Smile, Sadness! It's almost Christmas!"
Joy is trying her best to make Sadness smile.
Draw some colorful presents to cheer her up!

Joy watches one of Riley's happiest festive memories.

Christmas is Bing Bong's favorite time of year!
Brighten up this page with a Christmas tree
and lots of festive decorations.

Poppa shows Arlo how the fireflies light up the dark winter nights.

Arlo and Spot have a campfire to keep them warm in the snow.

Arlo and Spot look up at the snow
on the top of Clawtooth Mountain.

Spending time with family
is the best way to celebrate.

Arlo's favorite way to celebrate
is eating delicious food with friends!

Nash plays a happy tune on his bug harmonica.

Arlo can't wait to see his family!
Help him find the correct path back to Momma and the farm.